ATHENEUM BOOKS FOR YOUNG READERS · An imprint of Simon & Schuster Children's Publishing Division · 1230 Avenue of the Americas, New York, New York 10020 · Copyright © 2012 by Andy Runton · All rights reserved, including the right of reproduction in whole or in part in any form. · OWLY is a trademark of Andy Runton · ATHENEUM BOOKS FOR YOUNG READERS is a registered trademark of Simon & Schuster, Inc. · Atheneum logo is a trademark of Simon & Schuster, Inc. · For information about special discounts for bulk purchases, please contact Simon & Schuster Special Sales at 1-866-506-1949 or business@simonandschuster.com. · The Simon & Schuster Speakers Bureau can bring authors to your live event. For more information or to book an event, contact the Simon & Schuster Speakers Bureau at 1-866-248-3049 or visit our website at www.simonspeakers.com. · Book design by Sonia Chaghatzbanian · The illustrations for this book are drawn and inked by hand and painted using digital pastels. · Manufactured in China · 0812 SCP · First Edition · 10 9 8 7 6 5 4 3 2 1 · Runton, Andy. · Owly & Wormy, bright lights and starry nights / Andy Runton. — 1st ed. · p.   cm. · Summary: On a slightly scary camping trip to study stars in the night sky, Owly and Wormy make new friends. · ISBN 978-1-4169-5775-1 (hardcover) · ISBN 978-1-4424-5439-2 (eBook) · [1. Owls—Fiction. 2. Worms—Fiction. 3. Stars—Fiction. 4. Fear of the dark—Fiction 5. Night—Fiction. 6. Camping—Fiction. 7. Friendship—Fiction. 8. Stories without words.] · I. Title. II. Title: Owly and Wormy, bright lights and starry nights. III. Title: Bright lights and starry nights. · PZ7.R8882970u 2012 · [E]—dc23 · 2012010648

OWLY

Owly
& Wormy

BRIGHT LIGHTS
AND
STARRY NIGHTS!

ANDY RUNTON

ATHENEUM BOOKS FOR YOUNG READERS / NEW YORK • LONDON • TORONTO • SYDNEY • NEW DELHI